Seeing Zach

Written & Illustrated By
Bebe Kemper

With gratitude to Sue,
Leslie, Lynne, Judy, Heather, and
Mary — my unofficial "editors"
— but especially to Crosby,
for his faith and support.
B.K.

Timmy trudged along the sidewalk to his grandmother's house. He was glad she lived nearby because he loved doing art projects with her. Gram, that's what he called her, was an artist and she let Timmy share her paint and brushes. She didn't even mind when he got a little paint on the floor. "Because," she said, "being creative and having a good time is what my painting studio is for."

But today Timmy was even more glad that Gram was close by because she helped him feel better when he was sad. Right now, Timmy was feeling really sad because his dog, Zach, had died, and Timmy didn't know what to do about the hurt he felt from missing him. It was 'specially hard not to see Zach waiting for him when he got home from school. Zach was just about his best friend.

"Always try to understand, Timmy," Gram would say, "whenever you want something to get better, understanding is the thing you must try to find." Timmy hoped somehow she would help him understand.

As he pushed open Gram's squeaky front gate, Timmy saw her waiting for him on the porch. He knew she would have chocolate chip peanut-butter cookies for him — and even better, a big, warm hug.

They shared the hugs and a snack and then settled down on the porch swing with its plump and comfy pillows to talk. Gram held Timmy close and let him cry a bit.

"I'm never going to see Zach again," Timmy sobbed.

Gram was quiet for a moment, then she said, "Timmy, if you can understand the truth about Zach, if you can understand what Zach's real self is — the Zach you loved so much — then you can go on having what you loved about him with you always."

Gram could tell that Timmy was having trouble understanding, so she asked him, "Is it Zach's waggy tail and furry body, and big brown eyes that you miss the most about him, Timmy?"

He thought for a moment. "No," he sniffed. "I miss his love and ..." Timmy knew what he felt about Zach, but he just couldn't seem to find the right words.

"Let's talk about the ideas that are what Zach really is to you," said Gram, taking Timmy's hand. "I like to think of these ideas as God's qualities shining through Zach. The dictionary tells us that a quality is something that is special in a person or thing," she explained. "And, all of God's ideas, even animals, shine forth with God's special qualities."

Gram and Timmy talked about how special it was that Zach always loved him — even when Timmy forgot to take him along to soccer practice, or was a little late giving him his dinner when there was a lot of homework to do. Gram said that this kind of patient loving is called unconditional love — a big word that means loving each other no matter what.

"Weren't you always sure Zach loved you no matter what, Timmy?" asked Gram. "Yes," he agreed, "I was always sure."

They also remembered together how loyal, and gentle, and fun Zach was — and how he always seemed to know how Timmy was feeling.

"Timmy, "Gram went on in the gentle voice that made him feel better, "the things you love about Zach are qualities, or ideas of God, shining out from Him through your friend. And, because these ideas come from God and God will always be right where you are, Zach's ideas or qualities will always be right where you are, too, even if you can't see them. Can you understand just a little, that the things you love most about Zach have nothing to do with his furry body?"

Timmy nodded a wobbly nod, hesitantly, "But, I still wish I could hug him."

Gram understood how he felt. "Well," she told him, "you can learn to hug his qualities. You can look for them and feel them near you — everywhere, in everyone, even in yourself. You won't see them and touch them like you see and touch a furry body, but you will feel them very close, and it will feel good, and you won't be as sad. It may take a little practice, looking for these God-like ideas that are Zach's real self. But, when you find them, you will feel Zach with you. You will be 'seeing Zach'.

Timmy wasn't sure he truly understood how to do this, but he thought he'd try — for Gram. As he went out through her gate and looked back to see her waving good-bye, he felt a little better. He felt love right there with him. "Is that having Zach's love with me?" he wondered.

A few days later, Timmy was playing baseball in his back yard with some friends. He ran to catch a flyball and didn't watch where he was going. Suddenly, there he was running through Dad's garden, trampling down the tulips.

Timmy felt awful because it was such a pretty garden, and he also felt worried that he might be in trouble. But, when his dad came out of the house he put his arms around Timmy and said, "I know it was an accident. You love the flowers, too, and wouldn't want to hurt the garden. Just be more careful from now on." Together they picked up some of the tulips lying on the ground, and Timmy took them inside and put them in a vase for his mom.

Timmy didn't see it for a minute, but then he did. Dad loved him no matter what. That must be what Gram called **unconditional love** — just like Zach's love for Timmy! He was "seeing Zach" again!

On the Fourth of July
there was a big parade in town.

Timmy and his mom and dad stood on the sidewalk watching all the colorful bands with their shiny instruments and red uniforms marching by. There went Mr. Tuttle, the school bus driver, playing the big tuba and Mr. Long from the ice cream store was proudly carrying the American flag. His name fit him very well, Timmy thought, because Mr. Long was so tall.

Mom had bought little American flags for them to wave, and Dad said, "This is to show loyalty to our country."

"What does loyalty mean?" Timmy asked.

"It means being faithful and true to what you love and believe in," his dad told him.

"Gosh!" thought Timmy. "**Loyalty!** Like Zach's loyalty to me when he waited on the porch for me to come home from school." It seemed kind of like his friend, Zach, was right there at the parade with him.

One summer morning Timmy and his friend, Sadie, were lying on the grass watching the shapes the clouds made. Some clouds looked like trains, or cars, or animals. "Look, Sadie, that one looks like a dragon!

Timmy pointed to the cloud and as he did, a pretty orange and black butterfly landed very gently on his finger. Timmy was very quiet and still for a moment so he could be gentle back, and the butterfly would feel safe. He remembered how gentle Zach always was when he handed him a treat. Zach never snapped it up, but just took it gently in his mouth. Timmy was getting used to looking for Zach's ideas, or qualities — and here was another one — **gentleness** — right here with him.

But, something Timmy couldn't seem to stop missing about Zach was the fun they had together. It made him feel sad sometimes even when he was with his friends. One morning all the kids in the neighborhood were running through the lawn sprinkler to keep cool. They were laughing, sliding on the grass, and having lots of fun. "Come on, Tim!" shouted Sadie.

Timmy had been practicing looking for Zach's qualities and he wondered if he could see any of them now. He remembered that Zach was happy when he played in the water. Sadie's new puppy was rolling on the grass with her under the spray of water, so Timmy thought he'd try. Soon, he was having a happy time and it began to seem like Zach's **joy** was right there with them.

Gram had told Timmy that he could even find Zach's qualities in himself. But, he just didn't see how.

One evening Mom was doing the dinner dishes. She had been at work all day and Timmy thought she looked kinda tired. She had put on the big furry slippers she wore when her feet hurt. He decided to help out by drying the dishes. They sang songs, too, and were soon finished. Mom sat down and put her feet up. "Thank you, dear," she said with a smile. "How did you know that I was tired and needed help?"

"Because I love you," Timmy said softly.

Then, he remembered how Zach always knew how he felt — whether he was sad, or glad, or afraid. Sometimes Zach put his head on Timmy's lap as if to say, "I'm here to help." This time Timmy found one of Zach's qualities — **caring** — in himself, just as Gram had said he would.

Timmy was discovering that Gram was right. He was beginning to understand. If he really looked, he could find the special things about Zach, his spiritual qualities, everywhere — but he needed to remember to look.

He was beginning to understand that the things he loved so much about Zach would be with him always.

He could hardly wait to tell Gram how many ways he was "seeing Zach."